Mommy's Kisses and Cuddles

by
Linda Ashman

illustrated by
Jane Massey

Sun is rising,
Warm and bright.
Mommy lifts me,
Holds me tight.

We start our day
With a kiss –
Then another, just like this.

We make breakfast –
Mix and pour.
I add berries –
Then some more.

Drizzle syrup –
There, just right.
Open, Mommy – have a bite!

Mommy buttons, zips, and snaps.
Helps untangle twisted straps.

Ties my hat on with a bow.
One more hug, and off we go!

Mommy's calling, *On your mark . . .*
We go racing through the park.

Ride together down the slide,
Then we swing, side by side.

50
20
70

Through the market, holding hands,
Stop at all our favorite stands –

Plums and peaches,
Greens and beets.
Sit and share
Our tasty treats.

Me and Mommy on the mat.
I'm a tree.
She's a cat.

Stand and stretch
Like crescent moons.
Then we cuddle
Like two spoons.

Set the table,
Nice and neat.
Dinner's ready.
Time to eat!

Mommy asks about my day.
I have *lots* of things to *say*.

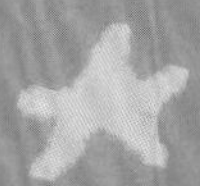

Mommy makes a soapy fin.
Adds a beard to my chin.

Dries me off.
Combs my hair.
Finds my jammies with the bears.

ABC

Mommy's reading – time to rest.
Lean my head against her chest.

One more book, then lullabies.
I hum along . . .
Then close my eyes.

Mommy rises, starts to go.
Softly whispers, *Love you so –*

Love each minute we're together.
Love you always and forever.